Harvey Green
the Eating Machine

Story by Gene Perret   Art by Gary Bennett

WitWorks™

WitWorks™
a funny little division of arizona highways books

2039 West Lewis Avenue, Phoenix, Arizona 85009
Telephone: (602) 712-2200
Web site: www.witworksbooks.com

Publisher — Win Holden
Managing Editor — Bob Albano
Associate Editor — Evelyn Howell
Associate Editor — PK Perkin McMahon
Art Director — Mary Winkelman Velgos
Photography Director — Peter Ensenberger
Production Director — Cindy Mackey
Production Coordinator — Kim Ensenberger

Library of Congress Catalog Number: 2001098991
ISBN 1-893860-78-7

FIRST EDITION, published in 2002.
Printed in Hong Kong.

Text © 2002 by Gene Perret
Illustrations © 2002 by Gary Bennett
Book design — Gary Bennett

Harvey Green
was an eating machine.
He ate everything in
sight.

Harvey Green was an eating machine. His appetite was **great.**

He'd eat everything that was dished out to him. He'd even swallow the **plate.**

Harvey Green was an eating machine.
He ate **fish...**

and
fowl...

and **meat.**

He'd slurp down his meal, burp, and then say, "Let's go out and get something to **eat.**"

Harvey Green was an eating machine. The most amazing thing he could **do** was eat 19 pies in a blink of an eye without even stopping to **chew.**

Harvey Green was an eating machine.
There's been no one like him **since.**
He ate spaghetti like licorice candy.

He ate pizzas like dinner **mints.**

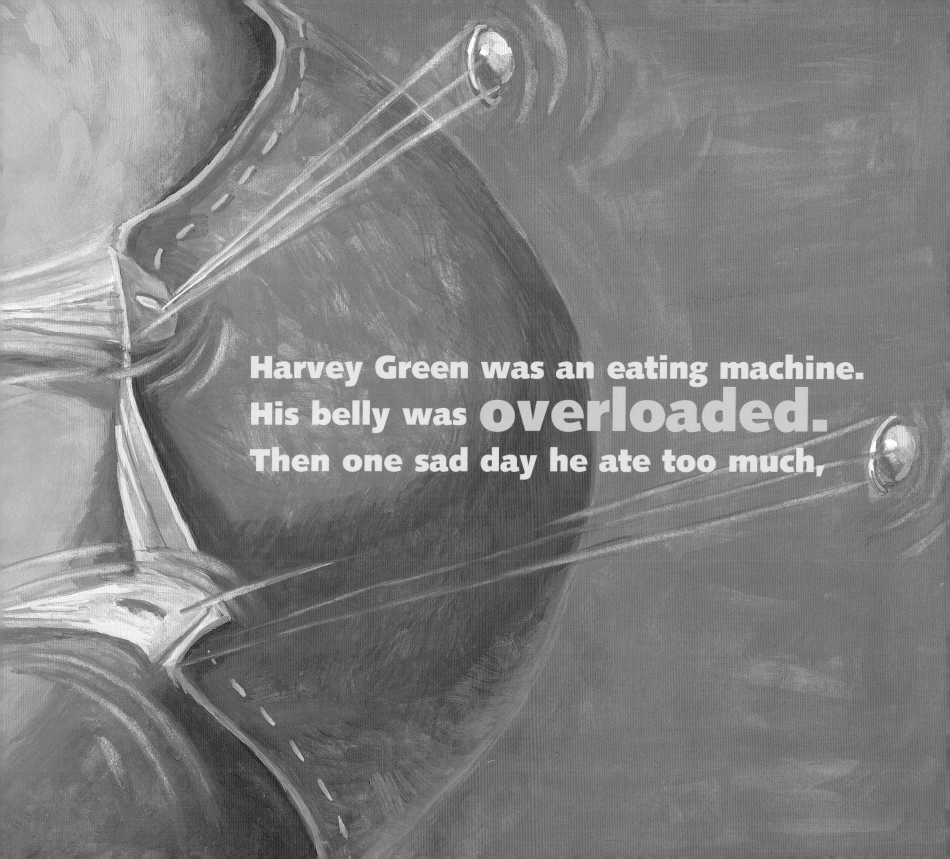

Harvey Green was an eating machine.
His belly was **overloaded.**
Then one sad day he ate too much,

No one knew what he should do,
not which, or what, or **whether.**
Then a kid named Freddy yelled, "Dinner
is ready."
And Harvey pulled himself
together.

HARVEY GREEN'S RULES

When you sit down to eat, you should never forget

behave with proper etiquette.

Chewing with your mouth closed is one place to begin.

Of course, you must open your mouth first to get the food in.

Chew your food slowly and quietly, too.

Or else you'll sound like a puppy munching a shoe.

Here's one rule that we should know.

The table's no place to rest your elbow.

TABLE MANNERS

Don't reach out and grab when your food's far away.

"Please pass the bread" is the right thing to

Saying "Please" and "Thank you" is good advice.

It's more than good manners; it's just being nice.

These are a few of the rules. There may be some others.

Oh yeah—don't throw potatoes at your

little baby